PECK'S TRAIL MIX
MIX-UP

Based on the episode written by Mike Kramer
Adapted by Annie Auerbach
Illustrated by Marco Bucci

ABDOBOOKS.COM

Reinforced library bound edition published in 2019 by Spotlight, a division of ABDO, PO Box 398166, Minneapolis, Minnesota 55439. Spotlight produces high-quality reinforced library bound editions for schools and libraries. Published by agreement with Disney Press, an imprint of Disney Book Group.

Printed in the United States of America, North Mankato, Minnesota.
092018   012019

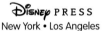 PRESS
New York • Los Angeles

THIS BOOK CONTAINS
RECYCLED MATERIALS

Library of Congress Control Number: 2017961156

Publisher's Cataloging-in-Publication Data

Names: Auerbach, Annie, author. | Kramer, Mike, author. | Bucci, Marco, illustrator.
Title: Sheriff Callie's Wild West: Peck's trail mix mix-up / by Annie Auerbach and Mike Kramer; illustrated by Marco Bucci.
Description: Minneapolis, MN : Spotlight, 2019 | Series: World of reading level pre-1
Summary: When Peck's favorite trail mix slowly starts disappearing, he decides to track down the trail mix thief.
Identifiers: ISBN 9781532141850 (lib. bdg.)
Subjects: LCSH: Sheriff Callie's Wild West (Television program)--Juvenile fiction. | Western stories--Juvenile fiction. | Sheriffs--Juvenile fiction. | Theft--Juvenile fiction. | Readers (Primary)--Juvenile fiction.
Classification: DDC [E]--dc23

Spotlight
A Division of ABDO
abdobooks.com

Peck loves trail mix.

It is the best snack.

Peck gets a new bag of trail mix.

"Hoo-wee!" he says.

Time for a snack!

Trail mix and milk.
Yum!

"Not now," says Callie.
Mr. Dillo needs help.

"Thanks, Peck! Thanks, Toby!"
says Mr. Dillo.

Peck helps his friends.

Good job, Peck!

Now Peck can eat his snack!

Oh, no! The bag is half empty!
Where did the trail mix go?

"Who is taking my trail mix?"
asks Peck.

Is it Mr. Dillo?
Nope!

Is it Priscilla?
Nope!

Is it Doc Quackers?
Nope!

Peck will find out!
He sets a trap.

Callie spots a hole in the bag.

But Peck does not listen
to her.

Peck hides.
He hears a *tap, tap, tap*.

The trap works!
But it does not catch the thief.
It catches Peck!

"Help!" says Peck.

Sheriff Callie and Toby come.

Callie shows Peck the hole.
The bag is leaking!

"We all make mistakes," says Callie.

Peck feels bad.

There is only one thing to do . . .

Peck gets a big bag of trail mix.
He will share with his friends.

"I'm sorry," says Peck.

Snack time for everyone!